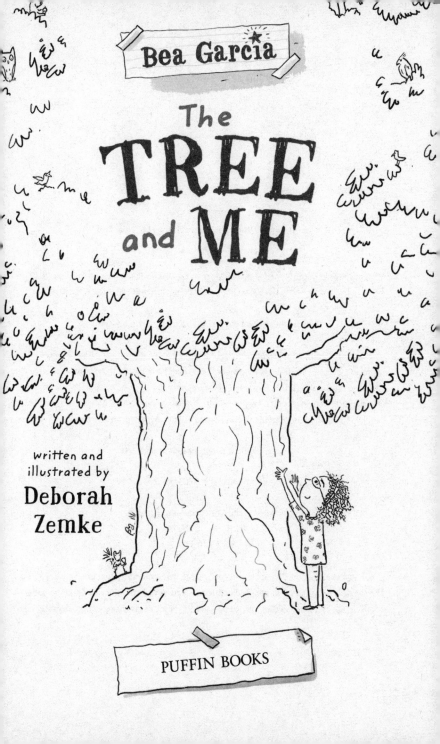

Bea Garcia

The
TREE
and ME

written and
illustrated by
**Deborah
Zemke**

PUFFIN BOOKS

PUFFIN BOOKS
An imprint of Penguin Random House LLC, New York

(penguin logo)

First published in the United States of America by Dial Books for Young Readers, 2019
Published by Puffin Books, an imprint of Penguin Random House LLC, 2019

Text and illustration copyright © 2019 by Deborah Zemke

Visit us online at penguinrandomhouse.com

Puffin Books ISBN 9780735229426

Printed in the United States of America
CIP Data is available.
3 5 7 9 10 8 6 4 2

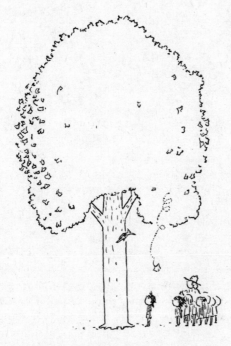

This story was inspired by the campaign of
Mrs. Schenker's class at Grant School to save the oak
tree outside their classroom window. It's dedicated
to all young authors, artists, and activists.

Chapter 1
INTRODUCING EMILY

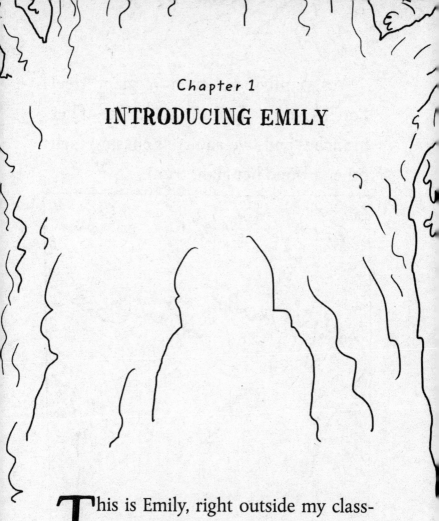

This is Emily, right outside my classroom window. She's so big that I can't fit her on one page.

Yes, Emily is a tree! A giant tree!
Look! There's a bird sitting on one of her
branches and two squirrels chasing each
other around her giant trunk.

This is me, Bea Garcia. I draw pictures of EVERYTHING.

I drew all the pictures in the book you're reading right now. Here's Zippy, one of the squirrels who lives on Emily.

See the skinny tail? That's how I can tell it's him.

Here I am at the top of Emily!

I WISH! I'm not really sitting high in Emily's branches, but wouldn't it be fun if I was? Sometimes I draw what I really see. Sometimes I draw what I wish I could see.

Do you see Zippy waving at you?

Imagine what I would see if I really were high in Emily's branches. The whole world.

Look! Way over there is Yvonne. She was my first best friend and lived right next door to me before she moved a million miles away to Australia.

Over here is my house. That's my mom and dad in the front yard. My mom draws pictures of houses, too. She's an architect.

In the backyard you can see my little brother, the Big Pest, throwing sticks for Sophie, the world's smartest dog.

I really do climb that crabapple tree in my yard. It's so tiny compared to Emily! The only thing I can see from its branches is Bert's yard next door. But let's not talk about him.

Here's my school, Emily Dickinson Elementary.

See that window? That's Mrs. Grogan's class. That's where I would be sitting if I wasn't up here in the tree.

Ignore the monster waving at the window. That's Bert.

Look down there on the playground!
My whole class is pointing up at me!

Fall? I'm not going to fall.

I'm going to FLY!

This is me, really. I'm sitting in the front row of Mrs. Grogan's class. I'm not high in Emily's branches. I'm not flying.

Everybody laughed except Judith Einstein, my new best friend and the smartest girl in the universe. That's her sitting right next to me.

If a man can be named Joyce then a tree can be named Emily.

I was doing just what the poem said. I was looking at a tree. Unlike Bert, who was being a monster.

Excellent, Bert. You've completed the next assignment before I even gave it. We'll all write short tree poems.

Bert—excellent? Bert is a monster. He can't be excellent, ever. Look at him. He calls me names.

He scares my little brother and my dog, Sophie.

He scares half the kids in Mrs. Grogan's class.

The other half thinks that he must be from another planet.

Another half thinks that Bert is cool. I know that's too many halves, but some kids think it's cool to be from another planet.

Bert's own mom told me that Bert likes being a monster.

He's a cryptozoologist.

That's a fancy way of saying he loves monsters. My mom told me:

Ignore him.

But Bert is hard to ignore, especially because he lives next door in the house where my first best friend, Yvonne, lived before she moved to Australia. Remember the picture I drew of my house? Here's Bert's next door.

There isn't really a "Beware of Monster" sign in his front yard, but there should be.

Bert took over Yvonne's house and now he's taken over this book, and I haven't even told you why I named a tree Emily or how I saved her life.

How we all saved her life.

Right. Judith Einstein is always 100 percent right. So let's start over.

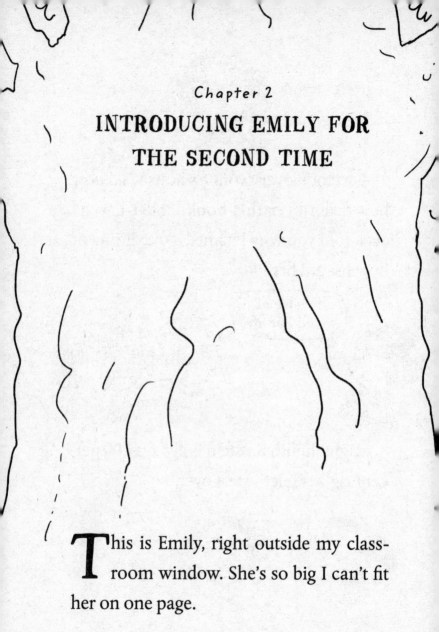

Chapter 2

INTRODUCING EMILY FOR THE SECOND TIME

This is Emily, right outside my classroom window. She's so big I can't fit her on one page.

Here I am, chasing squirrels around Emily's giant trunk!

I WISH!

Here I am, throwing acorns at Bert! He can't see me!

Now I'm flying high like a bird from the top of Emily!

ALMOST.

Here I really am, trying to write a short poem about a tall tree named Emily.

23

But first I'm going to tell you why we named a tree Emily. It wasn't just me. It was Einstein and me.

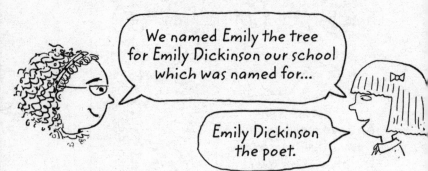

We named Emily the tree for Emily Dickinson our school which was named for...

Emily Dickinson the poet.

Einstein is probably the only kid in school who knows that Emily Dickinson was a poet. Or knows one of her poems.

"Hope is the thing with feathers..."

I'm not sure what that means, but it makes me think of flying.

Emily is the biggest tree on the playground. Every recess Einstein and I run to her. It's our secret meeting place even though it's right in plain view.

The other kids race off to play four square or basketball or monster tag (and yes, you-know-who is always It).

Einstein and I sit under Emily. Einstein reads while I draw pictures. Sometimes we talk.

Sometimes we get up and chase each other around Emily like squirrels.

Sometimes we play a game called Observe. Einstein always wins because she knows the names of everything.

But that's okay. I always win when we play Imagine. Here's what I imagine we look like to a nuthatch!

Sometimes squirrels throw acorns at us, especially Zippy.

But Emily always watches over us. It's like she's a big umbrella that protects us from sun and snow and … you-know-who.

At first we just called Emily *the* tree, but *the* didn't fit because if you look really closely, you can see . . .

a face! Do you see it?

Einstein says it looks like Emily Dickinson the poet.

Here I am, drawing a picture of Emily
the Poet Tree.

Mrs. Grogan looked at Einstein. She was
always ready first. Except this time.

Einstein still didn't raise her hand. She wasn't writing a short poem. She was writing a long list of *103 Top Tree Facts*.

Tommy's poem wasn't even about trees.

I liked Keisha's poem. It made me think of Emily.

You know I didn't have a poem to share. You know that instead of writing a poem I was drawing a picture.

Mrs. Grogan liked my picture.

I guess my Poet Tree wasn't quite the same as a poem because Mrs. Grogan gave me an A for imagination and a C for following directions.

Bert got an A for everything. He's never gotten an A for anything before. I think he should have gotten a big fat *zero*. And I think he should stop reciting his stupid poem.

I think Trees stink!

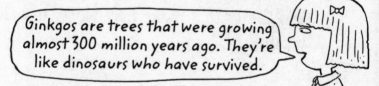

I asked Einstein what a gingko was. It didn't sound like a tree, it sounded like some kind of lizard. I was wrong.

> Ginkgos are trees that were growing almost 300 million years ago. They're like dinosaurs who have survived.

You can imagine what Bert thought of that. He loves monsters, and dinosaurs are the nearest things to monsters that have ever actually existed. Then Einstein made it even worse.

It's just the female gingko tree that smells bad.

Ginkstink! Just like girls!

Sometimes I wish Einstein didn't know everything. Sometimes that makes it hard to be her best friend. Especially when she says things that make Bert worse instead of just ignoring him.

You didn't ignore him either, Beatrice.

It's impossible to ignore Bert. But we all should have tried because everything that happened was his fault.

Chapter 3

IT'S ALL BERT'S FAULT

See? Here's Bert up in the branches of Emily. I'm not playing Imagine. And Bert's really not supposed to be there.

He's not all the way to the top. But he is high enough to look down at everyone on the playground. This is what we must look like to him. Mad.

We aren't mad at Bert because he climbed Emily. We're mad because he's throwing acorns at us like a silly squirrel.

At first he was just throwing them at
Einstein and me.

*That's Einstein's way of saying Stop!

*That's Spanish for Stop! But Bert didn't stop. When Keisha, Megan, Jackson, and Marcus ran over from playing four square to see what was happening, Bert threw acorns at them, too.

Everybody else raced over to see what was going on.

Bert threw acorns at all of them. Ben and Lauren picked up acorns and threw them back at Bert. The acorns bounced off Emily and hit Luis and Jacob, who picked up more acorns and threw them up at Bert. Soon everybody was throwing acorns.

It was an acorn war!!

Half the kids thought it was fun. The other half wished they could throw better.

But Zippy and his friends were terrified.
They started to hurl acorns, leaves, and
twigs at Bert.

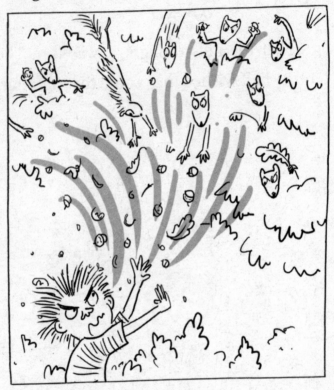

Everybody down below laughed except
Einstein and me.

And Mrs. Grogan, who ran over from the swings. She was so mad it looked like there was smoke coming out of her ears.

Everybody stopped, even Bert.

Bert didn't come down.

Bert still didn't come down.

He tried.

But ...

he couldn't.

STOP!

Bert stopped.

Principal Parker came running out of
the school.

Bert held on tight. We stayed back. We
heard sirens in the distance, getting closer
and closer.

Suddenly, Fireman Dave roared right up on the playground in his big noisy truck.

He was followed by KBOO-TV News.

We watched as Fireman Dave rode high up toward Bert in the rescue bucket.

Fireman Dave reached for Bert.

Bert held tight.

Bert didn't let go.

Bert let go.

Fireman Dave held tight. Everybody
cheered . . .

as Fireman Dave brought Bert safely down.

Everybody cheered but me.

Fireman Dave should have left Bert up there. Because if Bert hadn't thrown acorns at everybody then nobody would have noticed him.

If nobody had noticed Bert we wouldn't have had an acorn war, and Mrs. Grogan wouldn't have run over to stop it.

If Bert had come down when Mrs. Grogan yelled at him, then Principal Parker wouldn't have called Fireman Dave.

If Fireman Dave hadn't rescued Bert, then we wouldn't have been on TV and . . .

Lauren Winkleblinker's mother wouldn't have called up everybody else's parents.

58

Timber??!!!

My mom and dad told me . . .

They were wrong.

Chapter 4

I WON'T LET GO

The next day, just before we were about to go home, Mrs. Grogan told us the bad news. I mean she read the announcement.

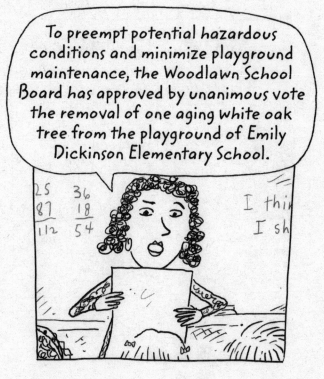

> To preempt potential hazardous conditions and minimize playground maintenance, the Woodlawn School Board has approved by unanimous vote the removal of one aging white oak tree from the playground of Emily Dickinson Elementary School.

No one understood anything except . . .

Einstein understood everything. She told me the bad news.

Here I am running out of the class . . .

out of the building ...

to the playground ...

where I spread my arms wide around
Emily.

I wasn't going to ever let her go.

Chapter 5

I WON'T LET GO, PART 2

The KBOO-TV news team came back, but I didn't let go.

Even though they made me seem silly I didn't let go.

Even though Fireman Dave didn't come to rescue me, I didn't let go.

68

I didn't let go when everybody waved on their way to the bus to go home or when the TV news team left.

I almost let go when Einstein had to leave.

Lying on top of all those acorns was re-ally uncomfortable, but I didn't let go. It was just me and Zippy and his friends.

And my mom.

And the Big Pest.

And Mrs. Grogan. Did she want to save

Emily, too?

I let go. I stood tall.

*Which means *Let's go home*, in Spanish. On the way I tried to think of how to save Emily. I knew I couldn't do it by myself. When we got home, my mom helped me call Einstein.

Chapter 6
HOW TO SAVE EMILY

Here we are, Einstein and me, sitting in the crabapple tree in my backyard. It's way smaller than Emily.

Einstein knows everything about trees. Almost. I taught her how to climb up here.

I used to play with my first best friend, Yvonne, in this tree. It didn't seem little then, it seemed magical. Yvonne and I used to play Imagine only we didn't call it that, we just called it playing.

Sometimes we played that the tree was
Mount Everest . . .

or the Pacific Ocean . . .

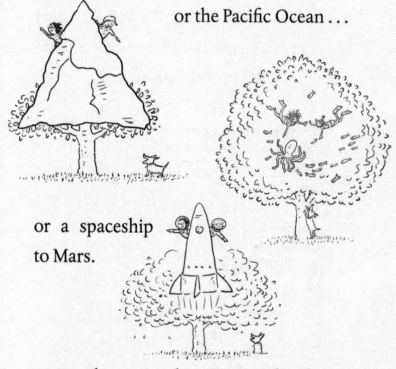

or a spaceship
to Mars.

But that was when Yvonne lived next
door, before she moved to Australia and
Bert moved in. See? Another thing that's
all his fault.

Einstein and I aren't playing anything. She's reading her plan to save Emily. Remember that list of *103 Top Tree Facts* that Einstein wrote instead of a poem? She rewrote it as *103 Reasons to Save Emily*.

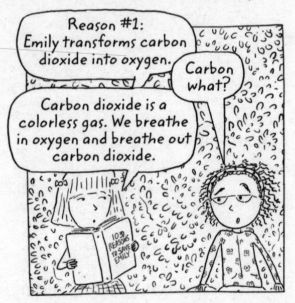

I didn't understand Reason #1. I didn't understand how it could save Emily. Then Einstein told me.

It sounded like magic to me. But was science the kind of magic that could save Emily? Einstein read Reason #2.

I couldn't imagine how candy that I wouldn't want to eat could save Emily. I just kept imagining Emily ... GONE.

I drew Emily the magician in Einstein's notebook. It was hard enough to draw sitting in a tree. Bert made it even harder.

Ignore him. He isn't really flying, he's jumping on his trampoline.

You can ignore my little brother, too. His real name is Pablo, but I call him the Big Pest because he really is one.

I observed. Do you see it? The T-shirt!

We all ran inside to make Save Emily T-shirts.

I drew the picture. Einstein helped to draw 2 million leaves. I'm just kidding, it wasn't that many.

The Big Pest made this scribble. He said it was a leaf.

Sophie helped, too. She brought us her favorite part of any tree.

My dad printed our picture on transfer paper, and we made three Save Emily T-shirts.

But could T-shirts and a stick save Emily?

Here I am, drawing 102 pictures plus the cover to save Emily.

Chapter 7
HOPE IS THE THING WITH FEATHERS

Here we are on the bus. We're on a See the Trees field trip to White Oak Heritage Arboretum, whatever that is.

An arboretum is a tree garden.

I think we should have stayed at school and had a Save Our Tree field trip on our own playground.

Or I could have stayed home to draw pictures for our plan to save Emily. I only had sixty-seven more to go.

Maybe we'll learn something that will help us to save Emily.

Maybe.

Welcome! I'm Ranger Ann!

Today we're going to learn about some fascinating flora— TREES!

I think trees stink!

Maybe if you-know-who wasn't in our group.

I WISH that Bert really could fly—far away, like to Mars.

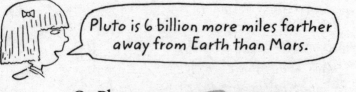

Pluto is 6 billion more miles farther away from Earth than Mars.

Or Pluto.

One of the best things about drawing pictures is I can send Bert to Pluto . . .

or make him disappear just like magic!!

I WISH.

I wish that Bert would just be quiet.

Here I am with my fingers in my ears so I wouldn't hear Bert as we walked around looking at trees with Ranger Ann.

You'll have to imagine everything since I can't draw any pictures with my fingers in my ears. There was a lot to see. Big trees, little trees, green, orange, and purple trees.

Here's a hickory and a hackberry.

Trees with bumpy bark and smooth bark and crinkly paper bark.

There's a sugar maple and a river birch.

We saw birds, too. Remember that upside-down bird on Emily?

A nuthatch!

There were squirrels and a really weird-looking critter . . .

that wasn't a critter. It was Einstein.

I looked.

It was Emily. Well, not Emily exactly, but a tree like her, tall and strong and reaching to the sky.

Emily was just as big and old and strong and beautiful and important as this tree.

Emily was saved!

Unless?

Unless the tree presents a danger, in which case it must be removed.

Emily wasn't saved. My heart sank to my knees and everything went quiet. It was funny how many sounds I had been hearing that I didn't even notice until they stopped—the birds, the wind in the trees, the squirrels. Bert.

Where's Bert?

I looked around. Where was Bert? He had disappeared, just like I had always wished.

ALMOST.

We followed Ranger Ann.

She followed the sound past orange trees with bumpy bark ...

and purple trees with crinkly bark ...

and green trees with red bark.

The sound got louder and louder . . .

until we came to a clearing.

There was Bert. He was looking up at
a golden tree, with his mouth wide open,
but no sound coming out.

The sound was coming from up in the
tree. Einstein passed me her binoculars.

Here's what I saw:

It looked like a dinosaur. Or Bert if Bert had bright red hair and black wings.

Ranger Ann whispered . . .

It's a pileated woodpecker.

We stared at the bird. It stared at Bert. Then Bert did something he'd never done before. He whispered.

The pterodactyl, I mean, the woodpecker, whispered back.

We all stood with our mouths open, but no sound coming out.

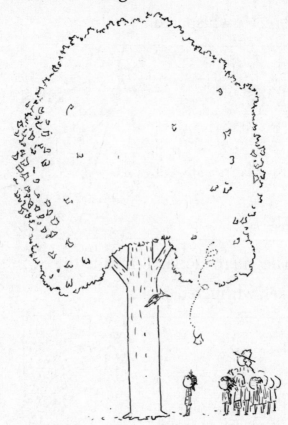

We watched one golden leaf drop from the tree, slowly swirling to the ground.

Then like magic, all the leaves fell like a golden snowstorm . . .

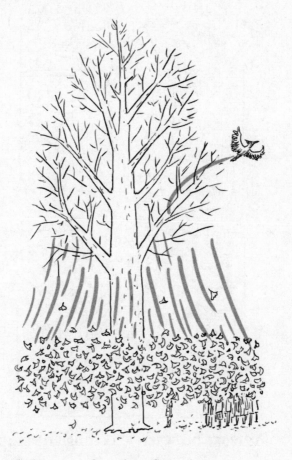

and the woodpecker flew away.

Bert didn't stay quiet long.

At least he wasn't reciting his stupid *I think trees stink* poem.

Chapter 8
EINSTEIN'S PLAN

Here I am waiting outside Principal Parker's office. Yes, that's you-know-who right beside me. He's been wearing his hair like that since we saw the pterodactyl, I mean, the woodpecker two days ago.

Mrs. Grogan told me that Principal Parker wanted to talk to me. I'm not in trouble.

Unlike Bert who has probably spent his whole life in trouble, sitting in that chair waiting to see the principal. Well, maybe not that exact chair since he just moved here, but a chair just like it, outside a principal's office just like Mr. Parker's.

What is Bert in trouble for this time? Climbing Emily? Starting an acorn war? Getting lost at the See the Trees field trip? Maybe it's for making noisy woodpecker sounds.

I shouldn't be sitting here with Bert. I should be sitting here with Einstein.

She wrote *103 Reasons to Save Emily*. She can explain how trees breathe and why Emily is irreplaceable. I just drew the pictures, not 103, but a lot.

We gave our plan to Mrs. Grogan who gave it to Principal Parker who asked to see us. Us—as in Einstein and me. But Einstein was at the dentist. I had to speak for Emily by myself.

Maybe NOT. But I had to try to save Emily. We all went into Principal Parker's office.

I told Mr. Parker why we named a tree Emily and how magical she was in a scientific way and that if Bert hadn't climbed . . .

If Bert hadn't flown into that tree and started an acorn war and been rescued by Fireman Dave, then nobody would have thought Emily was dangerous. Nobody.

Mr. Parker didn't say anything. He looked through our plan very, very slowly. Finally he looked up.

I did it! I did it! I DID IT! I saved Emily!

ALMOST.

My heart sank down into my shoes.

That wasn't Bert, that was me.

Chapter 9

HOPE IS THE THING WITH FEATHERS, PART 2

This is the fourth day in a row that Einstein and I wore our Emily T-shirts to school. Mine had peanut butter on the front and a paw print on the back. Einstein's looked brand new. She was sure we were on our way to saving Emily. I hoped that she was right.

I tried not to hate Lauren Winkleblinker. It wasn't her fault that her mom was a tree chopper.

Dear Mrs. Grogan's class,

The School Board will hear your request to cancel the removal of a tree from your playground.

You will have FIVE minutes at our next Board meeting on Wednesday, October 24, at 7:00 pm.

Until then, the playground will be

OPEN.

No one understood anything except . . .

Einstein understood everything. She told me the great news.

I was about to start dancing around my desk when it hit me. How could we save a 250-year-old tree in five minutes?

That didn't make anybody happy except Einstein and me.

We followed Mrs. Grogan out to the playground and over to Emily. There were still acorns everywhere.

I told them.

Here's everybody laughing . . .

except Einstein.

Einstein explained photosynthesis and
how we need trees more than they need us.

Yes! That was me talking about science!
And Mrs. Grogan talking about magic!

Mrs. Grogan showed more of the 103 reasons why Emily was so special.

And I showed them Emily's real face, not a drawing.

Everybody laughed again, but this time it was a together kind of laughter.

Mrs. Grogan's answer surprised me.

Then Tommy surprised me, too. He stepped forward and said ...

Keisha surprised me, too . . .

I am Emily.
I stand tall.

and Jacob . . .

I am Emily.
I eat the
sun.

and Adelaide.

I am Emily. I hold
the earth for you
to walk upon.

It sounded like poetry. Poetry for our
Poet Tree!

It sounded like poetry until . . .

it sounded like Bert. NO! Not again! Did
Bert climb Emily again?

Bert was right. It wasn't him. It was the pterodactyl, I mean the pileated woodpecker, in our Poet Tree, right on top of Emily's head.

It was like the bird had flown to our school to tell us, Save Emily!

The bird was the thing with feathers.
Hope.

And now that we had hope, we had
work to do! We all raced inside.

Everybody had an idea about how to help save Emily. Some kids wrote, some drew pictures, some danced. Bert sat like a quiet pterodactyl in his chair.

Here's what I saw when I looked out the window. Do you see it? Emily is smiling!

Just kidding! Trees may eat candy for breakfast, lunch, and dinner but they only smile in your imagination.

Chapter 10

I AM EMILY

The School Board meeting room was crowded with kids and their parents. Mrs. Winkleblinker called us up first.

My knees were shaking. My dad told me . . .

But I wasn't going to be myself.

I was going to be a 250-year-old white oak tree. A 250-year-old white oak tree with shaking knees.

Einstein was Emily, too, only her knees weren't shaking.

Tommy and Keisha were Emily, too.

So were Adelaide, Grace, and Tristan.

Fatima, Marcus, Megan, Jackson, Ben,

and Maria were all Emily.

Luis, Lailah, Jacob, Lucy, Trevon, and
Lauren were Emily, too.

Even Mrs. Grogan and Principal Parker came to save Emily. Everybody except you-know-who, which was a good thing.

We all stood tall and together.

When Ranger Ann stepped forward and named Emily an official State Heritage Tree, everybody in the room cheered.

Everybody except Mrs. Winkleblinker.

It was true—Lauren could get hurt climbing Emily. But Lauren had come up with another part of our plan to save Emily. Here she is, presenting our solemn promise.

Everybody except Bert signed.

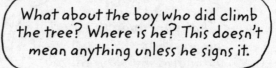

What about the boy who did climb the tree? Where is he? This doesn't mean anything unless he signs it.

I didn't think I'd ever want to see Bert until I saw him.

KAWK! I'm a pterodactyl!

Do you promise not to climb the tree?

Bert was Emily's last hope, the thing with feathers, even though pterodactyls didn't have feathers.

Would Bert promise? I had to do something. I whispered in Bert's ear a secret promise of my own.

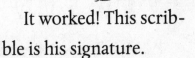

I will NEVER climb Emily. ok fyi

Bea
Lauren
Marcus
Lailah
Tommy
Luis
Fatima
Grace
Jackson
Adelaide

Judith
Trevon
Lucy
Megan
Leisha
Tristan
Ben
Jacob
Maria

It worked! This scribble is his signature.

If you can't read his writing, here's Bert on TV.

KAWK!!!*

*Which in pterodactyl means *I promise I won't fly into Emily.*

The Woodlawn School Board voted 7–1 to keep Emily.

We saved Emily!

ALMOST. Even signed solemn promises weren't enough for Mrs. Winkleblinker.

This is very nice, but what if somebody like Bert twenty years from now climbs Emily?

We stopped. There was a whoosh as if everybody's hearts had dropped to their knees. Then Mr. Parker made Mrs. Winkleblinker a secret promise of his own.

Chapter 11
WE ARE EMILY!

H ere we are, the whole class, spending our recess picking up acorns. It was Mrs. Grogan's idea, to clean up after ourselves. I don't mind at all.

I'm going to plant some of these acorns
in my own backyard and 250 years from
now I'll climb Emily Jr. and see all the way
to Australia. IMAGINE!

Yes, that's a fence around Emily. It was Principal Parker's secret promise to Mrs. Winkleblinker. Even twenty years from now somebody like Bert won't be able to climb Emily.

Mrs. Winkleblinker changed her vote to make it unanimous.

Unanimous means everybody agrees!

Painting pictures on the fence was my idea. That's Zippy and his friends, a nuthatch, a cardinal, and . . .

a pterodactyl. Who does it look like to you?

Yes, it's Bert.

That's the secret promise I made, to paint him as a pterodactyl. But I put him on the side where I wouldn't see him every day from the classroom window.

Now he's flying high around Emily forever. Well, not too high, and maybe not forever, but for a long time.

We really did save Emily, all of us kids. Even Bert helped—maybe more than anyone else. Don't tell him I said that. He *was* the one who found the thing with feathers.

Here we are, Einstein and me, sitting by Emily, outside the fence but still shielded by her strong arms. That's Zippy throwing an acorn at us. But just one. I think he was happy to see us.

THE POEM THAT
SAVED EMILY

I am Emily. I am your Poet Tree.

I turn carbon dioxide into oxygen for you
to breathe.

I am Emily. I stand tall. I reach to the sky.
I hold the ground for you to walk upon.

I am Emily. I clean your air. I feed your
earth.

I am Emily. I was here before you. I saw
you build this town and this school.

I am orange and green, red and brown. In
winter, I am bare.

I am Emily. I watch over you. I shield you from wind and snow, sun and rain.

I am Emily. I am home to Zippy and his friends. I am home to cardinals and robins, nuthatches and sparrows.

I am Emily. I have a hundred arms and thousands of fingers.

I am Emily. I eat the sun. I drink the earth.

I am a street from the earth to the sky.

I am Emily.

P.S. You could add to our poem or draw pictures to go with it. Or you could write your own poem about Emily. Or any tree. Or anything. Even a pterodactyl. You probably have already figured out that Bert didn't really fly into Emily. Look at page 37. He used Emily's head to climb up!